YUCK'S BIG BOOGER CHALLENGE
AND
YUCK'S SMELLY SOCKS

Illustrated by Nigel Baines

A Paula Wiseman Book
Simon & Schuster Books for Young Readers
New York London Toronto Sydney New Delhi

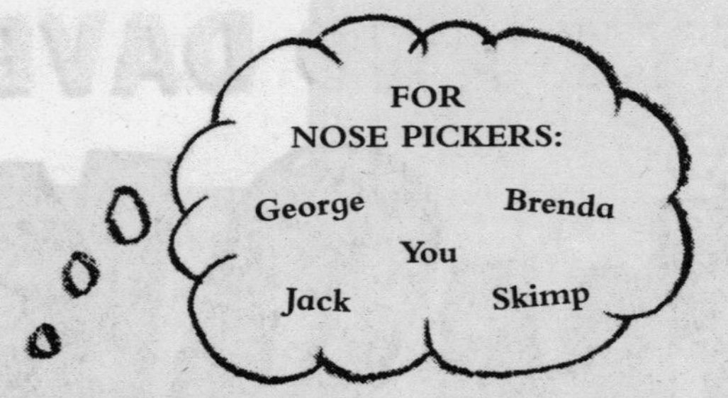

SIMON & SCHUSTER BOOKS FOR YOUNG READERS
An imprint of Simon & Schuster Children's Publishing Division
1230 Avenue of the Americas, New York, New York 10020

Originally published in Great Britain in 2006 by Simon & Schuster UK Ltd.

For information about special discounts for bulk purchases, please contact Simon & Schuster Special Sales at 1-866-506-1949 or business@simonandschuster.com.
The Simon & Schuster Speakers Bureau can bring authors to your live event. For more information or to book an event, contact the Simon & Schuster Speakers Bureau at 1-866-248-3049 or visit our website at www.simonspeakers.com.
Also available in a Simon & Schuster Books for Young Readers hardcover edition
The text for this book is set in Bembo Std.
The illustrations for this book are rendered in pencil and ink.
Manufactured in the United States of America
0513 OFF
2 4 6 8 10 9 7 5 3 1
Library of Congress Cataloging-in-Publication Data
Morgan, Matthew.
[Short stories. Selections]
Yuck's big booger challenge ; and Yuck's smelly socks / Matt and Dave ;
illustrated by Nigel Baines.
pages cm. — (Yuck)
"A Paula Wiseman Book."
Summary: In the first of two stories, Yuck makes a deal with his mother to stop picking his nose, making the whole family suspicious; and in the second, Yuck has a brilliant(ly disgusting) idea to make sure his mother never again nags him about wearing clean socks.
ISBN 978-1-4424-8311-8 (hardback) — ISBN 978-1-4424-8312-5 (paperback)
— ISBN 978-1-4424-8313-2 (eBook)
[1. Behavior—Fiction. 2. Nose—Fiction. 3. Cleanliness—Fiction. 4. Socks—Fiction.
5. Humorous stories.] I. Sinden, David. II. Baines, Nigel, illustrator. III. Morgan, Matthew. Yuck's big booger challenge. IV. Morgan, Matthew. Yuck's smelly socks.
V. Title. VI. Title: Yuck's smelly socks.
PZ7.M8254Yp 2013
[E]—dc23
yuckweb.com

CAUTION:
YUCKY FUN INSIDE!

YUCK'S BIG BOOGER CHALLENGE

"Stop picking," Mom said.

"I wasn't."

Mom looked around from the front seat of the car.

"Yes you were. I saw you."

"I wasn't doing anything," Yuck said.

Polly Princess was sitting next to him.

"You're disgusting, Yuck," she said.

Dad was driving. Polly reached over and tapped him on the shoulder.

Dad glanced in his mirror. "Yuck, stop picking your nose!"

Yuck wiped his finger on the car seat.

Just one more pick and . . .

"Use a tissue!" Mom told him.

"But Mom . . ."

Mom opened her handbag and rummaged for a tissue.

Yuck had just enough time to slip his finger up his nose.

Nearly got it. Just a little bit . . .

The booger was on the end of his finger.

The booger was in his mouth.

"Yuck! That's revolting!" Polly said. She turned away and looked out the car window.

Nice, Yuck thought, rolling the booger with his tongue.

"You are absolutely the most repulsive brother ever," Polly muttered.

Chewy, Yuck thought, pressing the booger between his teeth.

"Dad, did you see what Yuck just did?"

But Dad was busy driving.

Mom reached around from the front seat with a tissue in her hand. She pinched it over Yuck's nose.

"Blow," she said.

Yuck groaned.

"Yuck, do as your mom tells you," Dad said, turning the corner into their street.

Yuck huffed once into the tissue.

"Blow properly," Mom said.

Yuck huffed again.

"It's not fair," he complained as they pulled up at the house. "Why can't I pick my nose?"

"Because I said so," Mom told him.

Yuck decided that when he was EMPEROR OF EVERYTHING, everyone would have to pick their nose—it would be THE LAW. He'd collect all the boogers in a great big booger pit, and anyone found with a tissue would be dunked into it head first on a big booger bungee jump.

Mom opened the car door and marched Yuck to the house.

At home that evening, she kept a close eye on him.

She caught him picking his nose behind the sofa.

She caught him picking his nose in the tree house.

She caught him picking his nose in the closet under the stairs.

And when it was time for bed, she burst in on Yuck in his bedroom. He was hiding under the covers in the middle of an experiment, trying to get two fingers up one nostril. They were halfway up and about to pull out a long, stringy booger.

"Don't you dare!" Mom said, lifting his blanket.

Yuck groaned and pulled his fingers out slowly, trying not to snap the booger as it stretched. It pinged loose from his nostril. But just as he was about to eat it, Mom wiped his hand with a tissue.

"Skids!" Yuck swore. He'd been growing the booger for an hour.

"Put these on!" Mom said.

She handed him a pair of red mittens.

"But I'm not cold," Yuck told her.

"They're not for the cold. They're for nose pickers."

Yuck put the red mittens on. His fingers were trapped.

"They're itchy," he complained.

"They're to stop you from picking your nose."

Mom put a box of tissues by the side of Yuck's bed and went back downstairs.

But the red mittens were no match for Yuck. . . .

That night, he dreamed he was inside a nose as big as a cave. It was full of huge green booger boulders. He pushed one and rolled it away, and from underneath it two red snakes appeared. They coiled themselves around his hands. He pushed and fought, wrestling the snakes to the ground and rolling the booger boulder to the front of the cave.

In the morning he woke up sneezing. His nostrils were stuffed full with red wool. His fingernails were covered in woolly boogers. He'd picked his way right through the mittens!

Yuck wiggled his fingers.

"Rockits! What a pick!"

He hopped out of bed, threw on his clothes, and went downstairs for breakfast.

"What happened to your mittens?" Mom asked. She grabbed his hands and inspected them.

"It wasn't me," Yuck said. "It was moths—mitten-eating moths. They attacked in the night. They must have flown in through the window."

"You've ruined a perfectly good pair of mittens, Yuck!"

"Honest, Mom. It wasn't me. I've stopped picking my nose."

"He's lying!" Polly said.

"Really, Mom. From now on I'm using tissues."

Dad looked at Yuck and scratched his head. "What did you say, Yuck?"

"I'm never going to pick my nose again, Dad," Yuck promised.

"Don't believe him!" Polly said. "He's lying! Once a nose picker, always a nose picker."

"Not me," Yuck said.

From his pocket he pulled out a tissue and blew his nose on it.

"Well I never," Mom said.

"It's a miracle," Dad said.

"He's up to something," Polly whispered.

Yuck made a face at Polly and, as she went to eat a mouthful of cereal, he showed her the contents of his tissue.

"Go away! You're gross," Polly told him.

"It's okay, Polly, I know you're just jealous."

"Jealous? Why would I be jealous of you?"

"Because you want to share my reward."

"Reward?"

Polly looked at Mom.

Yuck quickly shook his tissue over Polly's bowl of cereal.

"That's right," Yuck said, sitting down in his seat. "My reward for not picking my nose for a whole week."

"And what's that, Yuck?" Mom asked.

"Candy!"

Yuck looked at Mom hopefully.

Mom looked at Dad.

"A whole week?" Dad said. "That's impossible."

"Okay, Yuck, one whole week of not picking your nose and you can have a jumbo scoop of candy from Candy Joe's," Mom said.

"Rockits!" Yuck said, pouring himself a bowl of Monster Snaps.

"But one pick and the deal's off," Dad told him.

"And what about me?" Polly moaned. "I don't ever pick my nose but I don't get a reward."

"You can have a scoop too, darling," Mom told her.

"Good. Then I'll get lots of candy and Yuck will get none because he'll NEVER manage to stop picking his nose!"

Yuck giggled. His nose twitched, and the Nose-Pick Challenge began. . . .

On Saturday morning, Yuck watched *Grossout!* on television. In the afternoon, he counted his scabs, and in the evening he won three extra lives on Skid Wars. All day his nose tingled, but he didn't pick it—just as he'd promised.

What no one knew was that he didn't blow it either. Yuck was a Boogerman with a Boogerplan—he was going to grow the world's biggest boogers! He'd get his candy and he'd get his revenge too—SWEET REVENGE!

All day the snot built in Yuck's nose, and that night his boogers began to grow. He dreamed he was in BOOGERLAND. He wore booger shorts and booger shoes, and snot instead of socks. He drove a booger car over booger roads and lived in a booger house. He had booger chairs and a booger bed and even a booger cat.

And everything was pickable!

By Sunday morning, a whole night's worth of gunk had collected in Yuck's nose. As the gunk dried, it turned crusty and began to itch. His Boogerplan was hatching.

All morning Polly Princess spied on him, desperate to catch him picking.

When everyone sat at the table to eat their Sunday lunch, Yuck noticed her watching him. He waited until Polly was looking, then pinched a pea between his fingers and slipped it into his mouth.

"Mom, Yuck just ate a booger. I saw him!" Polly said.

"No I didn't!"

Yuck opened his mouth for Mom to inspect.

"It's a pea," Mom said.

Yuck stuck his tongue out at Polly. "Serves you right for spying on me," he told her. And he grinned and went upstairs to his room.

That afternoon, Yuck busied himself by drawing a Booger Chart. In bright green pen, he wrote the days, 1 to 7, down the side of a piece of paper.

Next to day 1 he wrote TINGLY.

Next to day 2 he wrote ITCHY.

Suddenly he heard a knock.

"Is everything all right in there? Are you being good?" Dad asked from outside Yuck's door.

"I'm just blowing my nose," Yuck called.

He pretended to blow into a tissue, making a loud raspberry so Dad could hear.

"Only five days to go until Candy Joe's," Dad said.

Five days seemed a long time. But at least tomorrow, at school, there would be no one spying on him. At least that's what Yuck thought.

But on Monday, everywhere he went, Polly went too. Every corner he turned, there she was, spying on him in hallways, spying on him on the playground, spying on him in the cafeteria.

Juicy Lucy and Madison Snake were helping her. They giggled each time Yuck passed.

"Boogerboy," they whispered.

Yuck wanted to pick his nose and rub his boogers into their hair, but he stopped himself.

He had to stick to his plan. He didn't pick and he didn't blow. And his boogers kept on growing!

"Well, Polly?" Mom asked, when Polly and Yuck got home from school.

"Nothing," Polly said, disappointed.

"Hold out your hands," Mom said to Yuck.

Mom checked under his fingernails for boogers.

"Well I never. They're clean. I wouldn't have believed it if I hadn't seen it with my own eyes. That's three whole days without picking," Mom said.

Yuck stomped up to his room and gave his nose a scratch. He was desperate to pick it. It was filling up like he had a cold. With his green pen, next to day 3 on his Bogey Chart he wrote GOOEY.

GOOEY

By Tuesday, there was so much snot inside his nose that it was bubbling from his nostrils, pushing its way out like toothpaste from a tube. Mom tried to grab him and wipe it, but Yuck ran into the bathroom and sniffed the snot back in, then blew a raspberry into his tissue.

"All clean now," he lied.

And all day at school the spies were watching him as he sniffed.

He chewed his fingernails.

He had a lick of earwax.

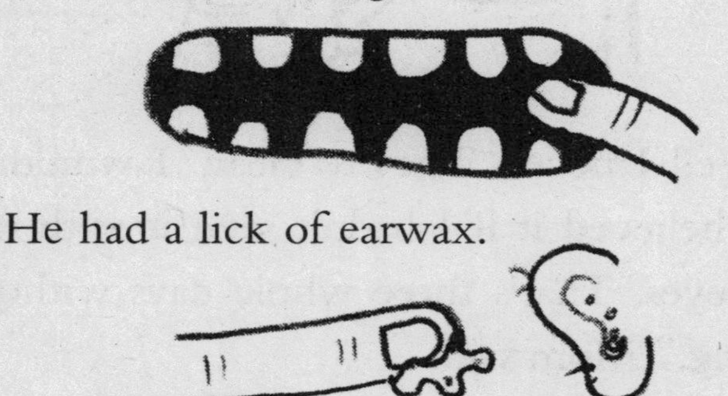

But he never picked his nose. He was determined to win.

And by the time he got home, his nostrils were so full that he had to plug them with modeling clay to stop the gunk from leaking out.

Next to day 4 on his Bogey Chart he wrote GUNKY.

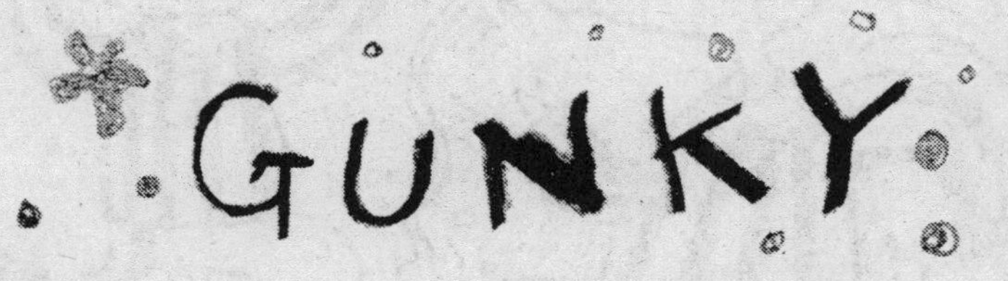

By Wednesday, day 5, his Boogerplan was taking shape. At the back of his nostrils Yuck could feel two lumps—two magnificent boogers growing in size.

He almost lost one of them playing soccer.

Frank the Tank was in goal. As Yuck shot to score, a booger the size of a brussels sprout dropped from one nostril. It hung on a string of snot three feet long.

Just as the string of snot was about to snap, Yuck gave an almighty sniff. The booger shot back up his nose like a yo-yo.

"Goal!" Little Eric shouted.

Next to day 5 on his Bogey Chart Yuck wrote STRINGY.

His plan was working.

By Thursday, his boogers were massive. He looked in the mirror. His nose was bulging on both sides, as if he'd stuffed socks up it.

"What's the matter with you?" Mom called to him as he ran out of the house.

"Bees. I got stung by nose-stinging bees," Yuck told her. "They must have flown in the window with the mitten-eating moths."

And all day at school he could hardly breathe through his nose, and his voice sounded funny when he spoke.

Polly and her spies teased him.

"Sore nose, Yuck? Dat's derrible. Why don'd you pick id?"

But Yuck didn't. He wanted his boogers to grow even bigger.

Next to day 6 on his Bogey Chart he wrote LUMPY.

Only one more day and SWEET REVENGE would be his!

That night, Yuck dreamed he met Candy Joe.

The candy captain was wearing black licorice shoes tied with strawberry laces and a fudge cap on his head. Candy Joe gave Yuck a gummy snake that wriggled in his hand. Fizzing saucers whizzed past Yuck's ears and chocolate bombs exploded all around him. He sledded, mouth first, down a mountain of ice cream, and splash-landed into a sea of caramel. . . .

It was CANDY-TASTIC.

Yuck woke with a smile and looked at his Booger Chart.

He knew exactly what he wanted to write next to day 7 . . .

IT WAS . . .

Just a few hours stood between him and SWEET REVENGE!

All day at school, Yuck stayed undercover.

He sat at the back in every lesson, hiding his nose in his hands. At lunchtime he hid in the boys' bathroom with his head under the faucet to stop his nose from exploding.

His boogers were massive—the world's biggest boogers!

When the bell rang and school was finally over, Mom came to collect him and Polly.

"Well, have you been good, Yuck?"

"I dink so," Yuck said, his nose swollen to the size of his fist.

"Anything to report, Polly?" Mom asked.

"Nothing," Polly replied, scowling. She hadn't caught Yuck picking all week.

Yuck held out his hands. Mom checked his nails.

"Well I never—absolutely booger free!" she said. "It looks like we're going to Candy Joe's after all."

"Roggits!" Yuck said.

Candy Joe's was the best sweet shop ever!

Yuck chose white chocolate splats and caramel bursts, toffee tongue-twisters and lemonade licks. He oohed and ahhed about which were best—shiny chocolate coins or sugar-dusted strawberry lollipops. He paused

over pear drops and puzzled over the butterscotch balls, dribbled over the peanut spirals and went loopy over the treacle whirls. He had one each of anything gummy and six of Candy Joe's special CANDY OF THE WEEK.

Driving back from Candy Joe's, he sat in the back of the car with chocolate around his mouth, and with his jumbo scoop of candy poured out across his lap.

Polly sat in the front seat next to Mom.

"Thank you, Mom," Polly said, picking a pink cherry heart from her scoop.

"Danks, Bom," Yuck said, scarfing a handful of fizzbees.

"You both earned it," Mom said. "I must admit, I never thought you'd be able to do it, Yuck."

"I dold you, Bom. I don'd bick by dose any bore. I use dissues," Yuck said.

He sucked on a triple-dipped chocolate finger, planning his revenge.

"Ooobbs, I've just drobbed by dissue," he said, ducking down behind Mom's seat.

It was time for the final part of his Boogerplan.

Yuck sniffed and snorted.

Out of sight of Polly and Mom, he had the biggest pick ever.

First he used one finger and then two. Then he used the stick of his loadsalollipop and then the spoon from his sherbet dunk.

Gradually he worked one sticky lump from the back of his nose to the front.

A huge booger burst out.

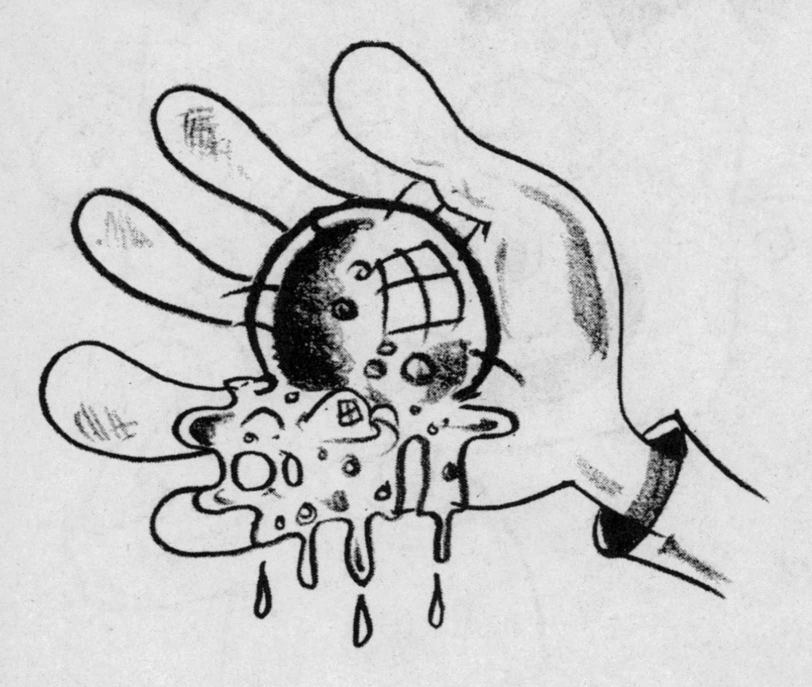

It throbbed in the palm of his hand.

It was enormous—a superbooger—the biggest, snottiest, stickiest booger that Yuck had ever seen. It was as big as a golf ball.

Yuck bent down again, pretending to blow into his tissue. He pressed one nostril closed and blasted the other.

A second booger shot out like a cannonball and splatted against the back of Mom's seat. Yuck scooped it off.

It was magnificent—just as big, just as snotty and just as sticky as the first.

Yuck rolled the boogers in his hands, round and round, until each one was shiny and smooth. All week he had been waiting for this moment.

He grinned.

"This is such a fantastic jumbo scoop of

candy," he said, sitting back up in his seat. "Especially the gobstoppers—they're the best!"

"Gobstoppers?" Polly Princess said. "I didn't see any gobstoppers at Candy Joe's."

"They were in a jar at the back," Yuck said. "SUPERSTOPPERS. The biggest and best gobstoppers in the world."

"SUPERSTOPPERS! That's not fair. I didn't get any. Can we go back, Mom?" Polly asked.

"Oh Polly, we're nearly home now."

"Please, Mom," Polly whined.

"Don't worry, you can share mine," Yuck told her.

"That's very kind of you, Yuck," Mom said. "How nice of you to think about your sister. Say thank you, Polly."

"Thank you," Polly mumbled.

"Would you like one too, Mom? They're ever so tasty," Yuck said.

"I'd love one, Yuck, thank you. It's been years since I had a gobstopper."

Yuck handed Polly and Mom one each—the two big green ones in his hands.

"They're huge!" Polly said.

"They're a lot stickier than I remember," Mom said.

"That's because they're SUPER-STOPPERS—the biggest and best in the world," Yuck said.

Mom opened her mouth and popped hers in.

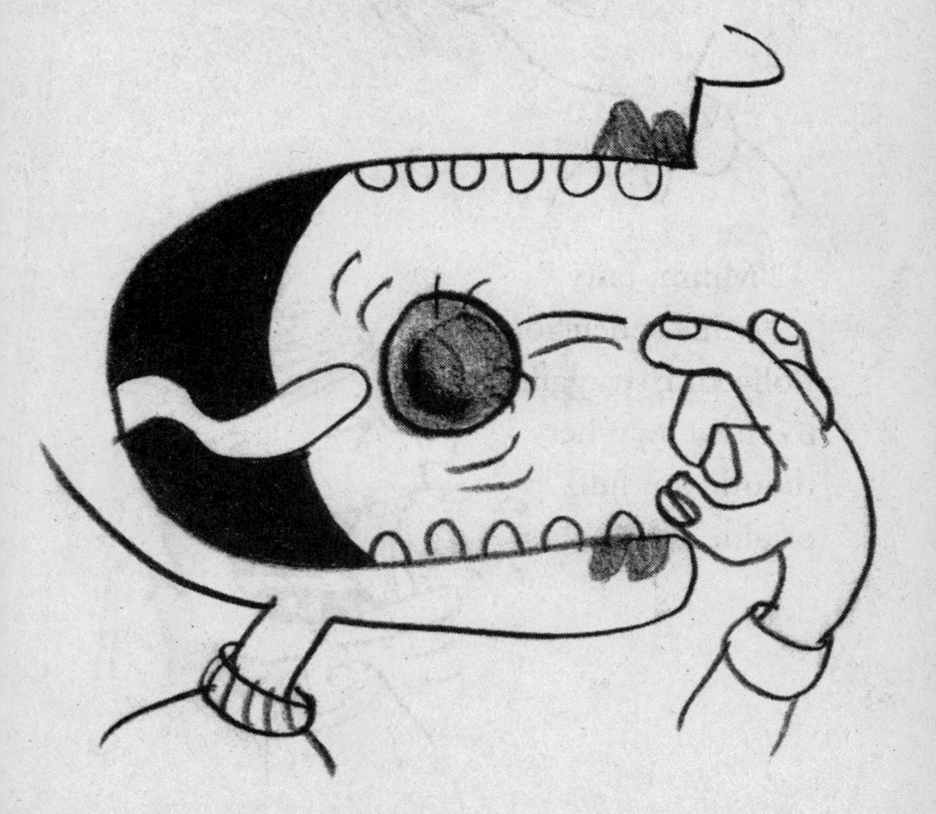

She sucked.

"Mmm, tasty."

"Mine's delicious," Polly said, struggling to chew, as if her mouth was full of glue.

Yuck giggled.
"That's because they're homemade."

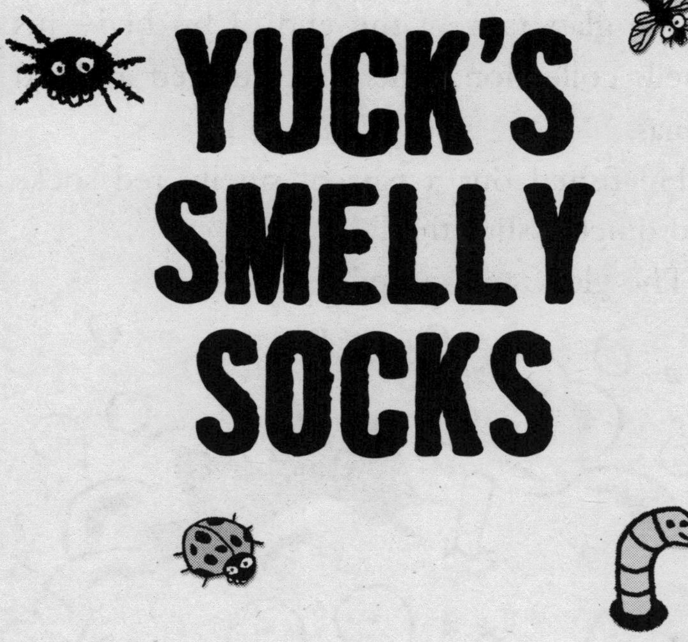

YUCK'S SMELLY SOCKS

Yuck opened his sock drawer—long socks, short socks, school socks, sports socks, and socks with holes. Socks of all different colors—some with stripes and some with spots. Some were in pairs and some were not. But every sock was CLEAN!

"Skids!" Yuck swore. "What's the point of clean socks?"

He closed the drawer and opened the lid of the glass tank at the end of his bed—his smells collection. The tank belched a cloud of gas.

He fished out a pair of smelly red socks and quickly shut the lid.

The glass tank rattled.

He pressed the smelly red socks against his nose and sniffed.

"Mmmmm . . . dirty, crusty, cheesy socks!"

He put them on.

Yuck decided that when he was EMPEROR OF EVERYTHING, all his

socks would be smelly. He would be the King of Foot Cheese and Toe Jam. And everyone would come from miles around to smell his feet. It would be the LAW!

"Have you got clean socks on today, Yuck?" Mom asked, poking her nose around his bedroom door.

"Yes, Mom," Yuck said.

Quickly, he ran past Mom and down the stairs to the front door.

Polly Princess was waiting for him. "Hurry up, I don't want to be late for school," she said. "Miss Fortune gives me stars for being on time."

"That's because you're a goody-goody," Yuck told her.

Yuck's teacher, Mrs. Wagon the Dragon, never gave him any stars.

Yuck picked up his bag and left with his sister, his socks wafting cheesy smells as he walked.

At the front of the classroom the Dragon was waving her umbrella.

"This week you are each going to write a poem," she said to the class.

Everyone groaned.

The Dragon checked that the tip of her umbrella was nice and sharp. "And at the end of the week you're going to read them out in front of the principal and the rest of the school."

"Do we have to, Mrs. Wagon?" Little Eric asked.

"Yes," the Dragon said.

She picked up a book from her desk.

"Here is the start of a famous poem by William Wordsworth," she said.

She began to read, "'I wandered lonely as a . . .'"

The Dragon pointed her umbrella at Schoolie Julie.

"What comes next?" she asked.

"Cheese!" Schoolie Julie said.

The class giggled.

"I wandered lonely as a cheese? Don't be ridiculous!" the Dragon said.

She waved the umbrella toward Megan the Mouth. "You!" she said. "I wandered lonely as a . . ."

Megan the Mouth covered her nose with her hand.

"Cheese!" she said.

The Dragon pointed her umbrella at Little Eric.

"Cheese?" Little Eric said, looking up.

The Dragon paused. Her nose twitched.

"Cheese!" she said. "I can smell CHEESE!"

"So can I!" Schoolie Julie said.

"So can I!" Megan the Mouth said.

"So can I!" the whole class said.

Everyone's noses were twitching.

The stench of strong, sweaty, smelly CHEESE was wafting from the back of the room.

Yuck was staring out of the classroom

window. His shoes were on the floor. His feet were up on his desk and his toes were wiggling in his smelly red socks.

"PHWOOOAAARRR!"

The class stared at him, sniffing.

"Yuck! Your socks stink!" the Dragon bellowed.

She marched over to him, holding her pointy nose with her fingers.

"Your socks smell like CHEESE!"

"Get those socks out of my classroom this instant!" she said, waving her umbrella.

The Dragon marched Yuck to the door.

"But they're my favorite socks, Mrs. Wagon," he said.

The Dragon handed Yuck a pencil and paper, and pushed him out of the classroom.

"No one wears smelly socks in my class! You can write your poem out there!" she said.

She made Yuck stand in the hallway, where no one could smell him.

"And it had better be good!"

The Dragon slammed the classroom door shut.

Yuck pressed his nose against the glass and watched. Everyone picked up their pencils and paper and started writing.

Yuck looked at the blank piece of paper in his hand. He picked his ear with his pencil. He couldn't think what to write.

I wandered lonely as a . . .

Poetry's boring, he thought. *Smelly socks are much more fun!*

Yuck had an idea, and he skidded off down the hallway and outside to the garbage cans.

Mrs. Wagon the Dragon was going to be in for a surprise. He was going to make the dirtiest, crustiest, smelliest socks in the whole wide world!

He lifted a garbage can lid and rummaged inside.

"Rockits!" He pulled out a moldy ham sandwich and half a banana.

Yuck stuffed the moldy sandwich into one sock and mushed the banana into the other, then squelched back inside.

He opened the door of Mr. Sweep the janitor's closet.

He looked along the shelves.

Floor polish? Oil? Soap? Grease?

Yuck took down the can of oil and the pot of grease. He squirted a long dribble of oil into one sock and dolloped a big scoop of grease into the other.

Then he skidded down the hallway and stood back outside the classroom, wiggling his toes until the end of the day.

That evening, in his bedroom, Yuck swept the dandruff and plastic spiders off his desk, turned his lamp on, and assembled his equipment—a spoon, his swimming goggles, and a baseball bat.

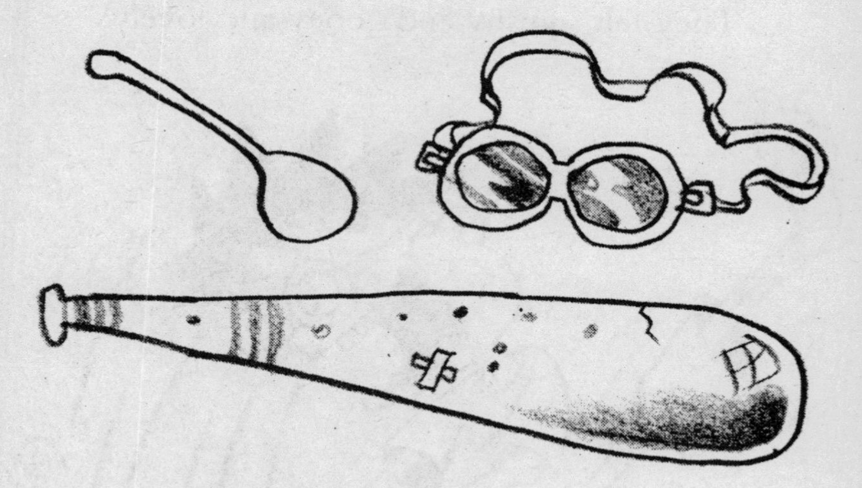

When everyone had gone to bed, he crept to the kitchen, opened the fridge, took out a block of cheese, and tiptoed back to his room.

Opening the lid of his smells collection, he grabbed his can of fart spray and sprayed some in his socks. Then he took out a rotten egg and placed it on his desk.

Swimming goggles on, he picked up his baseball bat and . . .

Yuck bashed the egg and the block of cheese until they were sloppy and mushy. He spooned them into his socks.

They felt squishy and gooey and lovely!

It was time to let it all stew.

He hopped into bed and wiggled his toes, feeling everything mixing together—the moldy ham sandwich, the mushy banana, the oil, the grease, the fart spray, the rotten egg, and the cheese.

With every wiggle, his socks became more and more dirty and smelly.

That night, Yuck dreamed he was in a factory with cheese going past on a long conveyor belt. He was Chief Hole-Maker, and he lay there dipping his toes into each block of cheese that went past.

The next morning, Yuck woke up and sniffed. Phwoarrr!

"Have you got clean socks on?" Mom asked him.

"Yes, Mom," Yuck said, running out the door on his way to school.

"I said no smelly socks!" the Dragon boomed. She was standing at the classroom door, pinching her nose.

"But they're my favorites, Mrs. Wagon," Yuck told her.

"I'll have no smelly socks in my class!"

She let all the other children in, then slammed the door.

From the hallway Yuck pressed his nose against the glass.

He watched as the Dragon walked around

the room seeing what everyone was writing. She waved her umbrella at Little Eric.

Yuck pulled the blank piece of paper from his pocket, chewed his pencil and thought for a second, then sneaked off to the school kitchens.

He could smell fish. Mrs. Dollop was preparing the school lunch. When she wasn't looking, Yuck tiptoed in and grabbed two fish sticks. He jammed one into each sock. Then he stuffed in a handful of cabbage and poured a bowlful of lumpy pudding and half a jug of cold gravy on top. It dribbled down his ankles and leaked into his shoes, sloshing up and down as he ran back down the hallway and stood outside the Dragon's classroom.

Cheesy, fishy socks!

Yuck wiggled his toes until dismissal.

"What did you do today, Yuck?" Mom asked when he got home that evening.

"We're writing poems," Yuck told her.

"I heard that you were sent out of class," Polly said.

Yuck buttered two slices of bread and took some more cheese from the fridge.

"I also heard that everyone else has nearly finished their poems and that you'll ALL be reading them out to the whole school at the end of the week."

"Megan the Mouth should keep her mouth shut," Yuck said.

"So what's your poem about, Yuck?" Mom asked.

"Or haven't you done it?" Polly said.

"It's a secret," Yuck told them.

He made himself a cheese sandwich, grabbed a bottle of ketchup, and went upstairs to his bedroom.

"Please, can no one disturb me?"

Yuck pinned a sign on his door saying POET AT WORK and wedged his chair under the door handle so no one could come in.

Opening his cheese sandwich, he peeled back the two slices of bread and sniffed.

"Mmmm . . . cheeeeeeese!"

He took his shoes and socks off, broke the cheese into little lumps, and wedged them between his toes.

With one slice of buttered bread in each hand, he wiped the butter over his feet, then stuck the slices together again with ketchup.

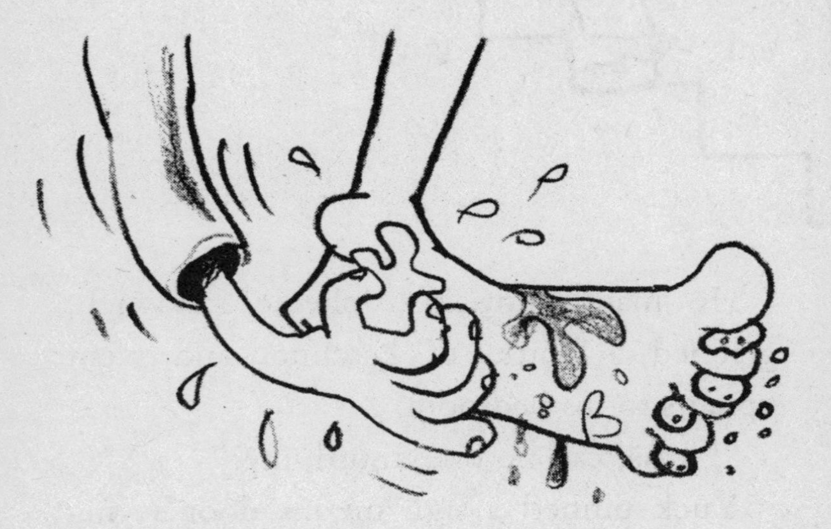

There was a knock at his door.

Yuck put his goggles on and picked up the baseball bat. . . .

"What are you doing in there?" Polly demanded.

"I'm writing my poem," Yuck said.

Polly rattled the door handle and pushed.

"Go away, Polly!"

Yuck spooned the soggy mess into his socks, slipped them back on, and hopped into bed.

Everything squelched as he wiggled his toes.

That night, Yuck dreamed he was at cheese school. The whole school was made of cheese. The doors were made of cheese, the desks were made of cheese, and the chairs were made of cheese. And when the Dragon waved her umbrella at him, it turned to cheese. Yuck ate it between two big slices of bread.

When he woke up, his socks were smellier than ever.

"Have you got clean socks on?" Mom called as he ran out the door.

"Yes, Mom," Yuck said.

But when he got to school . . .

"No smelly socks in my classroom!" the Dragon boomed.

Yuck stood in the hallway.

He waited until everyone was at their desks and the Dragon was walking among them, poking them, then he sneaked off down the hallway, out into the playground.

He ran to the school pond and scooped out a handful of frogs' eggs and stinky pond water. He poured it into one sock. Then he scooped out a handful of green slime and fish poo and slipped it into the other.

A frog hopped out of the pond.

"Ribbit!"

Yuck ran back and stood outside the Dragon's classroom, squelching in a pondwater puddle until the end of the day.

"What's for dinner?" he asked when he got home.

"Pizza," Mom replied.

"Rockits!" Yuck said, and he took an extra slice up to his room.

Wedging his chair behind his bedroom door, he set to work.

He took the slice of cheesy pizza and wiped it around his feet, getting the tomato sauce and cheese deep under his toenails.

There was a knock at the door.

"What's that smell?" Polly called. "I can smell something through the door."

"It must be your breath," Yuck said.

Just at that moment, a frog hopped out of one of his socks.

"Ribbit!"

"And what was that noise?" Polly asked.

"Go away, Polly!"

The frog flicked its long tongue and licked Yuck's cheesy toes, covering them with frog spit.

"Good boy," Yuck said.

He picked the frog up and put it on his desk.

He put his goggles on and picked up the baseball bat.

The frog croaked.

Yuck wiped a piece of ham sandwich from the bat and gave it to the frog to eat. "Don't worry, I'm not going to hurt you."

And as Yuck slipped his socks on and hopped into bed, the frog hopped after him and licked his toes while he slept.

That night, Yuck dreamed he was paddling in the sea.

He dipped his toes in the water, and all the fish jumped out, shouting, "Phwoarrr! Cheesy!"

When he woke, his socks were slimier and smellier than ever.

That day, there was a note waiting for him on the classroom door.

NO SMELLY SOCKS!

Rockits! Yuck thought.

He sneaked off and, in the bushes by the school gate, found two slugs, some bird poo, and some cat puke. Phwoarrr!

He dropped a slug into each sock, then wiped the bird poo and the cat puke over his toes.

When he got home, he went to the kitchen cupboard and fetched a pot of extra-hot mustard, an onion, some garlic, and a bag of cheesy crisps. He took everything up to his room.

A little later, there was a knock at his bedroom door.

"What's going on in there?" Polly asked. "It smells very cheesy."

"I'm writing my poem," Yuck said.

"No you're not. And tomorrow you're

going to be in BIG TROUBLE when Mrs. Wagon finds out."

"Go away, Polly!"

Yuck added a spoonful of extra-hot mustard to each sock, then put on his goggles, picked up his baseball bat and . . .

He crushed the onion, the garlic, and the crisps into tiny pieces and sprinkled them over his toes.

He pulled his socks back on and hopped into bed.

Yuck wiggled his toes—everything felt nice and sweaty.

He heard a "Ribbit!" from under the blanket and felt a long wet tongue flick over his ankles.

"Good night," Yuck said to his frog.

That night, Yuck dreamed he was in a land where everything was stains and smells. He met cheesy people with garlic hats and farting dogs and crusty cats . . .

When Yuck woke up, he threw back his blanket and a cheesy cloud erupted from his socks. They were ready! The dirtiest, crustiest,

smelliest socks in the whole wide world!

"Are you wearing clean socks today?" Mom asked when she saw him.

"Yes, Mom!" Yuck replied, and he ran out the door.

On the way to school, Yuck passed two dogs that were sniffing each other's bottoms. When they saw him, they ran over, sniffed his socks, barked, and ran away.

My socks smell worse than a dog's bottom! he thought. *This is going to be fun.*

But when he arrived at school, the Dragon was waiting for him.

In her hand she was holding a pair of CLEAN socks!

"But, Mrs. Wagon!" Yuck said.

"Put these on!" she told him, and she dragged Yuck to the assembly.

"I hope you've written your poem. We're all waiting to hear it."

Everyone was sitting on the floor.

The Dragon walked to the stage. Mr. Reaper the principal was standing at the front. "Today, Mrs. Wagon's students are going to read us their poems," he announced to the school.

"Who would like to go first?"

No one put their hand up.

"Come on—don't be shy!"

Little Eric hid behind Yuck.

"What's that smell?" Little Eric asked.

"Yuck!" the Dragon called. "Yuck will go first!"

Polly was sitting at the front with Juicy Lucy. She grinned as Yuck was made to walk through the crowd to the front of the room.

He stepped up onto the stage.

"I'm pleased to see you are wearing clean

socks today, Yuck," the Dragon said, grinning.

Yuck looked down at the clean socks on his feet, and walked to the center of the stage.

His hands were in his pockets, fumbling for something.

He pulled out a piece of paper.

"My poem is called . . ."

The piece of paper was blank.

"What's that?" Polly whispered to Lucy.

"Yuck's poem."

"No, not that. Look!"

Yuck was wearing something red on his hands.

He sniffed and smiled. "My poem is called . . . 'I Wandered Lonely as a Cheese.'"

The Dragon looked at the Reaper. The Reaper's nose twitched.

Yuck sniffed his hands and smiled.

"I wandered lonely as a cheese,
To a land of smelly make-believe,
Where (as this pungent poem tells),
Everything was stains and smells."

"Why is he wearing gloves?" Lucy asked.

Polly squinted. "Those aren't gloves! Those are his smelly socks!"

Yuck was sniffing, making up his poem from the different smells:

"Cheesy people and garlic hats,
Farting dogs and crispy cats,
Banana shoes and slugs for treats,
Pond-water puddles and gravy streets."

Polly rushed to the front.

"He's wearing his smelly socks on his hands!"

The Dragon looked at Yuck. "Yuck—!"

But as she opened her mouth to speak, a great cloud of cheesy gas wafted from Yuck's smelly socks and she swallowed it.

"Cabbage houses and pizza stairs,
Oily tables and greasy chairs,
Moldy picnics and onion pies,
Fish-stick grass and frogs' eggs skies."

The children in the front row coughed.

The Dragon leaned against the Reaper to steady herself. Her tongue was lolling out of her mouth. Her eyes were rolling.

"Uuurgh!" she screamed, breathing in the thick cheesy cloud as it billowed through the room.

"Ketchup cars and eggy trains,
Fish-poo boats and bird-poo planes,
Mustard ponds and custard lakes,
Frog-spit drinks and cat-puke cakes."

Slowly, the thick cheesy cloud drifted across the children. They felt dizzy. They began to sweat.

Polly sniffed.

"Get him off!" she cried, but when she opened her mouth, the cheesy gas went in.

Polly fainted.

"Evacuate the building!" the Reaper gasped.

"Keep going, Yuck!" Little Eric called out.

"Stains and smells were everywhere,
Noses sniffing cheesy air,
But much more smelly than all these things,
Were my smelly socks, so they made me KING!"

The cheesy cloud from Yuck's socks floated up to the ceiling, then all at once, water started pouring down.

Yuck's smelly socks had set off the sprinklers!

"Poetry's canceled!" the Reaper called, dragging the Dragon out of the room by her ankles.

The children coughed and cheered.

Yuck smiled and took a bow, and everyone crawled out of the room spluttering. All of them were soaking wet.

Then came the sound of a siren.

It was a fire engine, come to find the source of the poisonous gas.

Mom got quite a surprise when she heard the doorbell and opened the front door to see a fireman in a gas mask, holding Yuck's smelly socks in a plastic bag.

"I think these need washing, ma'am," the fireman said. He handed the smelly socks to Mom.

Yuck stepped out from behind the fireman.

"Thanks for the ride, mister," he said.

And he stepped inside.

Mom closed the door.

"YUCK!"

Then the doorbell rang again. This time it was an ambulance driver. Polly was standing beside him, wrapped in a blanket. She was coughing and spluttering.

"They've evacuated the school because of a poisonous gas," the ambulance driver said.

Polly stepped inside.

Mom closed the door.

"Yuck! These are going in the washing machine NOW!"

She was holding his socks, pinching her nose. "They're disgusting!"

Yuck followed Mom into the kitchen, took one last sniff, and watched as Mom opened the door of the washing machine and threw his smelly socks inside.

But just as she was closing the door on the front of the machine . . .

"Wait a minute, Mom," Yuck said. "I've got some more."

"More!"

Yuck ran upstairs.

"I want every last pair!" Mom called up after him.

Yuck ran to his room and fetched all the clean socks from his sock drawer. He ran back into the kitchen with his arms full of socks and stuffed them all in the machine.

"You're disgusting, Yuck," Mom said.

"From now on, it's clean socks EVERY day!"

She closed the door of the washing machine, picked up a box of Supersuds laundry detergent and poured some in the top. Then she poured in some more—just to make sure.

"Cleans all known stains and smells," Yuck read on the box.

We'll see about that, he thought.

He crossed his fingers.

When the Supersuds was in, Mom turned the machine on to FULL POWER.

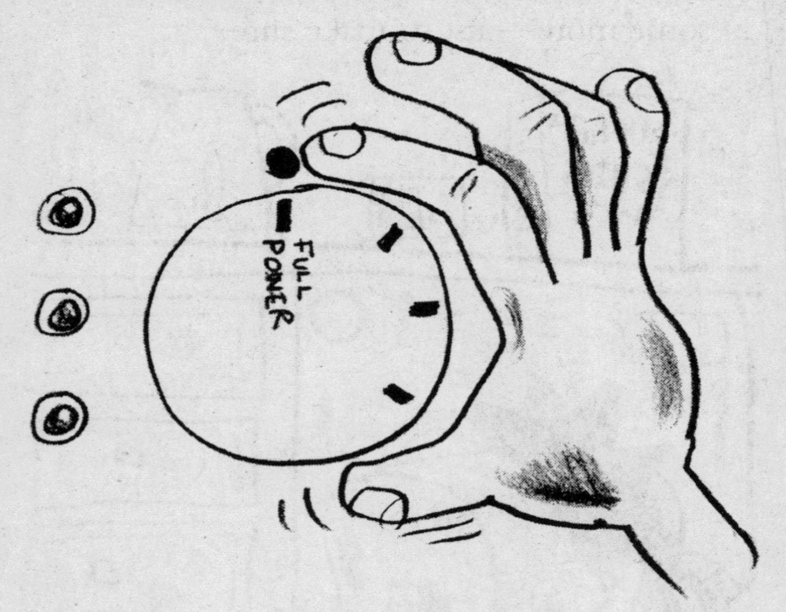

Yuck, Mom, and Polly stood in front of the washing machine and watched. The machine filled up with water and started to whirl.

The Supersuds foamed.

The machine made noises.

It growled.

It groaned.

Yuck's socks spun faster and faster.

The Supersuds and his smelly socks were locked in battle.

Yuck could see lumps of cheese, pieces of fish stick, and bits of cat puke spinning round and round.

The Supersuds frothed. The water started bubbling and boiling.

Yuck saw bird poo, frogs' eggs, and pizza.

The machine was whining and gurgling.

"What's happening?" Polly asked.

"Supersuds can clean anything," Mom said.

But at that moment there was a huge clang—then a crunch. The machine stopped.

Mom and Polly looked at each other.

The door of the washing machine sprang open, belching a thick cloud of cheesy gas.

"UUURRRGGGHHH!" Mom and Polly cried.

Yuck reached in and pulled out his socks. He took a big sniff and smiled.

"Rockits!"

Now all his socks were smelly!

"Nothing beats my smelly socks!

For yucky videos, yucky jokes, and lots of yucky fun visit yuckweb.com.

YUCK'S AMAZING UNDERPANTS

YUCK'S SLIME MONSTER

YUCK'S FART CLUB

YUCK'S PET WORM